P9-DLZ-669

**FRED BEAR and FRIENDS**

# FIRST DAY AT School

By Melanie Joyce



**WEEKLY READER®**
**PUBLISHING**

Please visit our web site at www.garethstevens.com
For a free catalog describing our list of high-quality books, call 1-800-542-2595 (USA) or 1-800-387-3178 (Canada).
Our fax: 1-877-542-2596

Library of Congress Cataloging-in-Publication Data

Joyce, Melanie.
First day of school / Melanie Joyce. — North American ed.
p. cm. — (Fred Bear and friends)
Summary: Betty makes many new friends on her first day of school.
ISBN-13: 978-0-8368-8971-0 (lib. bdg.)
ISBN-10: 0-8368-8971-1 (lib. bdg.)
ISBN-13: 978-0-8368-8978-9 (softcover)
ISBN-10: 0-8368-8978-9 (softcover)
[1. First day of school—Fiction. 2. Schools—Fiction. 3. Teddy bears—Fiction. 4. Toys—Fiction.] I. Title.
PZ7.J8283Fir 2008
[E] — dc22 2007031185

This North American edition first published in 2008 by
**Weekly Reader® Books**
An Imprint of Gareth Stevens Publishing
1 Reader's Digest Road
Pleasantville, NY 10570-7000 USA


First published in Great Britain in 2007 by ticktock Media Ltd., Unit 2, Orchard Business Centre, North Farm Road, Tunbridge Wells, Kent, TN2 3XF United Kingdom

Gareth Stevens Senior Managing Editor: Lisa M. Guidone
Gareth Stevens Creative Director: Lisa Donovan
Gareth Stevens Art Director: Alex Davis
Gareth Stevens Associate Editor: Amanda Hudson

Photo credits (t=top, b=bottom, c=center, l=left, r=right, bg=background) All photography by Colin Beer of JL Allwork Photography except for Shutterstock: 23tl.

Every effort has been made to trace the copyright holders for the photos used in this book, and the publisher apologizes in advance for any unintentional omissions. We would be pleased to insert the appropriate acknowledgements in any subsequent edition of this publication.



Printed in the United States of America

1 2 3 4 5 6 7 8 9 10 09 08 07

# Meet Fred Bear and Friends

Betty

Jess

Also starring...

Dolly

Alice

Today is Betty's first day at school. She is very excited.

"You will love school," says Fred.

Fred, Arthur, and Jess walk to school with Betty.

Betty sees her friend Dolly at school.
Dolly is starting school today, too. Dolly
and Betty meet their new teacher, Miss Jones.

Betty hears a bell.

**Drrring!**

The bell means
school is about
to begin.

Betty walks
into the school.

Betty hangs up her coat.
Then she sits down.

Miss Jones calls each
student's name.
"Betty?"
"Here, Miss Jones,"
answers Betty.

The first lesson is about shapes.

Betty and Dolly practice counting shapes. Betty counts the blue shapes on the board. “One, two, three, four,” she says.

The bell rings again.

**Drrring!**

It is time for recess.
Everyone goes
outside to play.

Betty and Dolly make
two new friends.

Their names are
Max and Alice.

"Would you like
to play a game?"
asks Alice.

Betty, Dolly, Max, and Alice play together at recess. Dolly loves to play hopscotch.

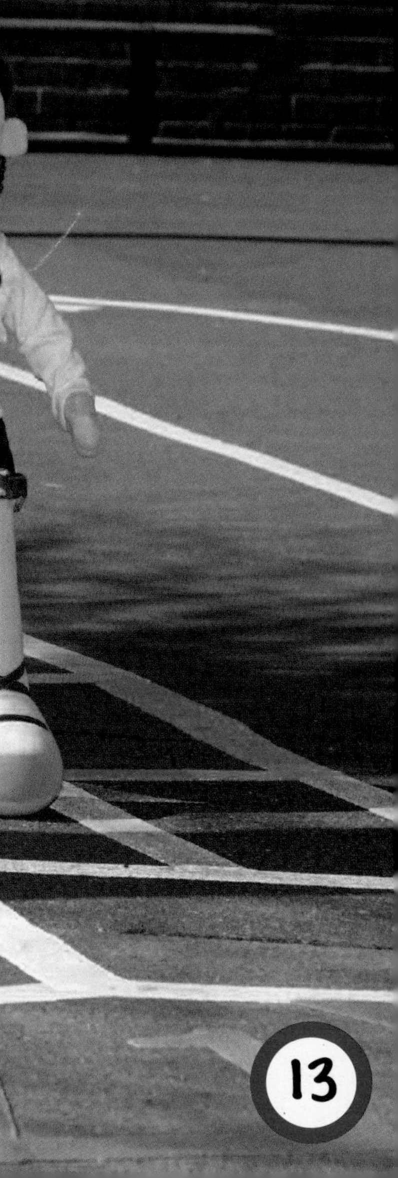

**Fred Bear says...**

Recess is a great time to make new friends and to play games.

Recess is over.
The class goes
to the gym.

The class plays a game.

After the game, Betty
feels hungry. Now it
is lunchtime.

Max, Dolly, and Betty sit
at the lunch table.

After lunch,
Betty and Dolly
write in their
workbooks.

Later in the day,
Miss Jones reads a
book to the class.

Betty listens closely
to the story.

The bell rings.

**Drrring!**

It is time to
go home.

Jess, Arthur,
and Fred are
waiting for
Betty at the
school gate.

They walk
home together.

The bears play school at home. Betty is the teacher.

Betty is excited to go back to school tomorrow.

"I love my new school," says Betty. "I had fun and made new friends!"

# Match the Shapes

Betty learns about these shapes at school.

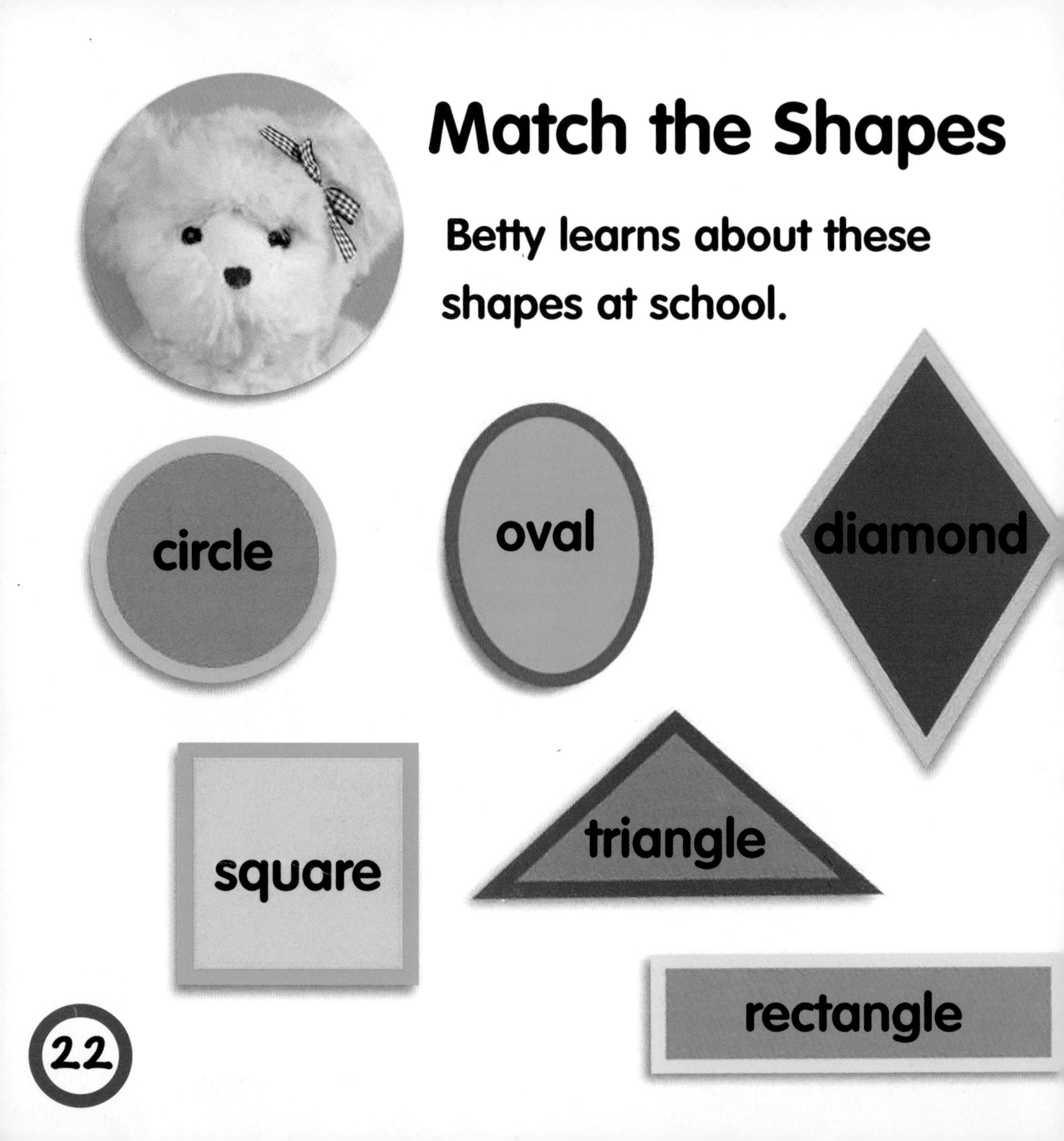

Here are items Betty saw at school and at home. What shapes are they?

sandwich

book

soccer ball



ANSWERS: The sandwich is a triangle. The book is a square. The soccer ball is a circle.

# Match the Numbers!

Dolly loves to play hopscotch at recess. Match the white numbers to the numbers on the hopscotch board.